ENCYCLOPEDIA BROWN

Solves Them All

Encyclopedia Brown books published by Lodestar

Encyclopedia Brown, Boy Detective   No. 1

Encyclopedia Brown and
the Case of the Secret Pitch   No. 2

Encyclopedia Brown Finds the Clues   No. 3

Encyclopedia Brown Gets His Man   No. 4

Encyclopedia Brown Solves Them All   No. 5

Encyclopedia Brown Keeps the Peace   No. 6

Encyclopedia Brown Saves the Day   No. 7

Encyclopedia Brown Tracks Them Down   No. 8

Encyclopedia Brown Shows the Way   No. 9

Encyclopedia Brown Takes the Case   No. 10

Encyclopedia Brown Lends A Hand   No. 11

Encyclopedia Brown and
the Case of the Dead Eagles   No. 12

Encyclopedia Brown and
the Case of the Midnight Visitor   No. 13

Encyclopedia Brown's Book of Wacky Crimes

No. 5

ENCYCLOPEDIA BROWN
Solves Them All

by DONALD J. SOBOL

illustrated by Leonard Shortall

DUTTON CHILDREN'S BOOKS

For
My Son
Eric

Library of Congress Catalog Card Number: 68-22746
ISBN 0-525-67212-5

Published in the United States by Dutton Children's Books,
a division of Penguin Young Readers Group
345 Hudson Street, New York, New York 10014

Published simultaneously in Canada by McClelland & Stewart, Toronto

Printed in the U.S.A.
30 29 28 27 26 25 24

1.   *The Case of the Missing Clues*   7

2.   *The Case of the Super-Secret Hold*   17

3.   *The Case of the Wagon Master*   25

4.   *The Case of Sir Biscuit-Shooter*   32

5.   *The Case of the Frightened Playboy*   40

6.   *The Case of the Hair Driers*   48

7.   *The Case of Cupid's Arrow*   56

8.   *The Case of the Wounded Dog*   64

9.   *The Case of the Earthenware Pig*   72

10. *The Case of the Muscle Maker*   79

The Case of the Missing Clues

Although there are thousands of private detectives in the United States, the town of Idaville had but one.

Idaville did not need more. Its one detective was Encyclopedia Brown, and he had never lost a case.

Aside from Encyclopedia, Idaville was like most towns its size. It had three movie theaters, two delicatessens, and four banks. It had rich families and poor families. It had churches and synagogues, and a lovely beach which everyone could use.

And for more than a year, no grown-up or child had got away with breaking the law.

Encyclopedia's father was chief of the Idaville police. People across the country believed he was the best police chief in the world.

Chief Brown was proud of his record. He was proud of his men. But he was proudest of his only child, Encyclopedia.

Alas, Chief Brown had to keep his pride in Encyclopedia a secret. Whom could he tell? Who would believe him? Who would believe that the real mastermind behind Idaville's war on crime was ten years old!

Whenever the police came up against a puzzling case, Chief Brown knew where to go. He went home. Encyclopedia would solve the case during dinner in the Brown's red brick house on Rover Avenue.

Encyclopedia never whispered a word about the help he gave his father. He didn't want to seem different from other fifth graders.

But he was stuck with his nickname.

Only his parents and teachers called him by

his real name, Leroy. Everyone else in Idaville called him Encyclopedia.

An encyclopedia is a book or set of books filled with all kinds of facts. Encyclopedia had read more books than anyone in Idaville, and he never forgot what he read. He was the only library in America that could get around on a two-wheeler.

Between schoolwork and police work, Encyclopedia kept busy during the winter. During the summer he ran his own detective agency. He solved cases for the children of the neighborhood.

Every morning during the summer he hung his sign outside the garage:

BROWN DETECTIVE AGENCY
13 Rover Avenue
Leroy Brown, President
No case too small
25¢ per day
plus expenses

Early one afternoon a small boy pulled a red wagon into the Brown Detective Agency.

The wagon was loaded with fresh fruit. The boy was loaded with anger.

He slammed twenty-five cents onto the gasoline can beside Encyclopedia.

"My name is Abner Nelson," he said. "I want to hire you. I sell fruit."

"Is business dropping off?" said Encyclopedia.

"No, it's disappearing!" said Abner. "For the past two weeks a big kid comes to my stand every day. He helps himself to whatever he likes. And he doesn't pay!"

"You need protection," said Encyclopedia.

"Protection!" screamed Abner. "Oh, no! I want to be *protected* from protection!"

Abner explained. He grew the fruit in his back yard and sold it at a stand on Grant Road. Two weeks ago a big kid had stopped at the stand.

"He told me I needed protection," said Abner.

"From whom?" asked Encyclopedia.

"From other boys who have fruit stands during the summer," replied Abner. "The big kid said they might wreck my stand."

"So he offered to protect you?"

"Yes," said Abner. "He comes by every day with a big grin and brags about what a swell job he's doing of protecting me. 'Nobody has bothered you, right?' he says. Then he takes something to eat for his services."

"He's protecting you clean out of business," said Encyclopedia.

"I never needed him. He fooled me with his fast talk," said Abner. "You've got to stop him before he eats me into the poorhouse."

"What's his name?" said Encyclopedia.

"Bugs Meany."

"I might have guessed!" said Encyclopedia.

Bugs Meany was the leader of a gang of wild older boys. They called themselves the Tigers. They should have called themselves the Berries. They were always getting into one jam after another.

"That Bugs is awful tough," said Abner.

"Don't be afraid," said Encyclopedia. "I've dealt with him before. Let's hear what he has to say for himself."

"He won't say anything about the bag of cherries he took an hour ago," said Abner glumly.

The Tigers' clubhouse was an unused tool shed behind Mr. Sweeny's Auto Body Shop. When Encyclopedia and Abner arrived, Bugs was alone.

The Tiger leader was getting ready for school. He wasn't studying a book. He was studying a bicycle lock. He was teaching himself to open it with a hairpin.

Seeing Encyclopedia, he hastily shoved the hairpin into his pocket. "Make like a tree and leave," he snarled.

"First pay Abner here for all the fruit you've lifted from his stand," said Encyclopedia.

"You owe me three dollars and a quarter," said Abner. "And forty cents for the bag of cherries you took an hour ago. I never needed your protection!"

"What's this? Protection? Bag of cherries?" cried Bugs. "Say, you two guys better not walk too close to a candy factory. They're looking for nuts like you."

Encyclopedia picked up a paper bag from the floor beside Bugs. Inside were three cherries.

"Where did you get these cherries?" demanded the boy detective.

Bugs worked hard at appearing calm. "Wh-why, I bought a pound of them at the supermarket this morning."

"You mean you helped yourself to a pound from my fruit stand an hour ago!" said Abner.

"Listen," growled Bugs. "I've been right here in the clubhouse all afternoon, eating cherries and thinking. I don't know anything about protection, a fruit stand, or *your* bag of cherries."

"If that's true," said Encyclopedia, "you won't mind if I look around."

"Go right ahead," said Bugs. "Search till your eyeballs blister."

Encyclopedia ran his fingers over every inch of the floor.

The search did not take long. The clubhouse was tiny. The only bits of furniture were a carved up table and six orange crates which the Tigers used for chairs.

Encyclopedia got down on his hands and knees. He ran his fingers over every inch of the floor. He found seven nails, a clothes hanger, two comic books, three dried leaves, and a half inch of dirt and dust.

Next he turned to the wood box which the Tigers used as a wastebasket. It held two more comic books, an old newspaper, a rusty belt, and a broken checkerboard.

When Encyclopedia was finished with the wastebasket, he went outside.

Again he got down on all fours. He circled the clubhouse, digging his fingers into the grass and weeds. He touched every bit of ground for ten feet around the clubhouse.

Abner knelt beside him. "Are you looking for clues?"

Encyclopedia nodded, but did not reply.

"What did you find?" Abner pressed.

Encyclopedia opened his hand. "This," he said. On his palm were a piece of string, a paper clip, and several bubble-gum wrappers.

"There's nothing else around but plain old earth, grass, and weeds," said Encyclopedia.

Bugs sat down in the clubhouse doorway. He plucked a long stalk of grass and chewed on it triumphantly.

"Well, now, Mr. Brains," he said. "Did you find what you were looking for?"

"No," answered Encyclopedia. "And that proves you weren't in the clubhouse all afternoon!"

WHAT MISSING CLUES
PROVED BUGS LIED?

(*Turn to page 87 for the solution to the Case of the Missing Clues.*)

The Case of the Super-Secret Hold

The heart of Bugs Meany was filled with a great longing.

It was to knock Encyclopedia flatter than an elephant's instep.

Bugs hated being outsmarted by the boy detective. But whenever he felt like throwing a punch, he remembered Sally Kimball.

Sally was the prettiest girl in the fifth grade. It wasn't her face, however, that the toughest Tiger remembered. It was her fists.

Sally had done what no boy under fourteen had even dreamed of doing. She had outfought Bugs Meany.

Bugs told everyone that Sally had hit him with

a few lucky punches. Nobody believed his story, including Bugs himself. He thought she had hit him with a milk truck.

Because of Sally, Bugs never bullied Encyclopedia. Sally was the detective's junior partner.

"Bugs hates you more than he hates me," Encylopedia said as the partners sat in the Brown Detective Agency one afternoon. "You can be sure he'll try to get even."

Sally agreed. "He's like a thermometer in hottest Africa," she said. "He's always up to something."

Just then Duke Kelly, one of Bugs Meany's Tigers, entered the garage. He put twenty-five cents on the gasoline can. "Bugs wants you," he said.

"He wants to *hire us?*" gasped Sally.

"No, he wants you to come to the judo show this afternoon," said Duke. "The twenty-five cents will pay for your time."

Encyclopedia and Sally exchanged questioning glances.

"The judo show starts at two o'clock in the junior high school gym," said Duke.

"Judo?" Encyclopedia repeated half to himself. "The gentle art of self-defense?"

"Judo is the art of using your opponent's strength against him," said Duke, "or her."

With that he departed, grinning slyly.

"Bugs has more up his sleeve than his elbow," said Encyclopedia thoughtfully. "But I'm curious."

"So am I," said Sally. "Let's find out."

The junior high school gym was already filled with boys and girls when the detectives arrived. Coach Richards, who ran the summer sports program, spoke briefly. He explained the aims of judo.

Then four men from the Idaville Judo Center took places on the mat in the middle of the floor. They wore white trousers and a loose jacket bound at the waist by a knotted belt. For half an hour they demonstrated holds, locks, throws, and escapes.

After the children had stopped clapping, Coach Richards spoke again.

"Judo is not only for grown-ups," he said. "Three of our own junior high school students will now show you what they have learned in two short weeks."

Bugs Meany and two of his Tigers, Spike Larsen and Rocky Graham, trotted onto the mat. They wore the same white costumes as the men.

"Gosh, he's really good," said Sally as Bugs began flipping Spike and Rocky to the mat like baseball cards.

"They know how to fall without getting hurt," said Encyclopedia. "But the throws are an act. Bugs couldn't toss Spike and Rocky if they didn't let him."

After a whirlwind five minutes, the Tigers lined up and bowed. Coach Richards stepped forward to thank them.

Bugs held up his hand. "I'm not finished," he said.

Coach Richards moved back, surprised.

Bugs repeated the grip on Rocky.

Spike strode toward Bugs. He stopped within a foot of his leader.

Bugs shot a hand to Spike's throat. When he pulled the hand away, Spike fell over on his back and did not move.

Bugs repeated the grip on Rocky. He, too, fell over on his back and lay unmoving.

"You just saw my super-secret hold," announced Bugs. "I completely knocked out Rocky and Spike. But I didn't hurt them. If I really wanted to, though, I could break their necks for life."

Rocky and Spike stirred. They crawled off the mat shaking their heads.

The gym had grown silent. All eyes were on Bugs.

"Now you're asking yourselves, 'Where did Bugs learn this terrible hold?'" he continued. "I'll tell you. I wrote to a famous professor in Japan for the secret."

Bugs strutted up and down the mat. "A lot of you have heard about a certain girl who is supposed to have licked me," he went on. "Now you know I wasn't trying. I could have put her in the hospital, only I'm a gentleman."

His meaning was clear, and all the children understood. Bugs was challenging Sally to a rematch, then and there! If Sally refused to fight, or if she were beaten, Bugs would rule the neighborhood. The Brown Detective Agency would be powerless to halt his bullying.

A small boy near Sally pleaded, "Don't fight him. He could *kill* you!"

But Encyclopedia whispered into Sally's ear. As she listened, her lips tightened. "Super-secret hold, phooey!" she snorted. A moment later she was on the mat.

Bugs turned white. He had thought to scare her. Now *he* was the one who was scared.

There was nothing for him to do but fight. He reached for Sally's throat and took a thump in the stomach.

Fortunately for Bugs, his two-week course in judo had taught him how to fall. Sally's fists gave him plenty of practice. Eventually he lay on his back and refused to get up.

"I can't go on," he wailed. "I hurt my back lifting a big box this morning."

"He must have hurt his head," thought Encyclopedia, "to believe anyone would fall for his super-secret hold!"

WHY DIDN'T ENCYCLOPEDIA BELIEVE THE HOLD?

(*Turn to page 88 for the solution to the Case of the Super-Secret Hold.*)

The Case of the Wagon Master

"Sssh!" whispered Sally. "I think we are about to be attacked."

Encyclopedia listened. He heard a faint rustle of leaves outside the Brown Detective Agency. But he could see no one.

"It must be Joe Cooper," he said quietly.

For a long time nothing happened. Then a voice barked, "Bang! Bang!"

From behind the bush jumped a boy dressed like Daniel Boone. He wore a suit of buckskin, a coonskin cap, and moccasins with colored beads. He was aiming a rusty old rifle at the detectives.

"Joe Cooper!" scolded Sally. "You shouldn't go around scaring people like that!"

"I'm on the warpath," announced Joe.

Joe came from one of Idaville's oldest families. The Coopers had settled in the area when it was still overrun by palmetto palms and Indians. Whenever Joe felt mad at anybody, he went "on the warpath." He dressed up like a frontiersman and pretended to shoot his enemy. It made him feel better.

"I could have filled you both with holes," he said proudly.

Encyclopedia knew Joe's rifle was so old and rusted it couldn't shoot gumdrops. "I'm glad you missed," he said, playing along.

"I missed you on purpose," said Joe. "It's not you I'm mad at today. It's Buck Calhoun."

"Holy cats!" exclaimed Encyclopedia. "Buck Calhoun has been dead for a hundred years. You can't shoot *him!*"

"Of course not! What do you think is making me so mad?" shouted Joe. Then, in a calmer voice he said, "Did you see the story about him in the newspaper this morning?"

Encyclopedia nodded. The newspaper re-

"I want to hire you," Joe said.

ported that a statue of Buck Calhoun had been unveiled at Fort Hope. The statue honored Buck's quick thinking in saving a wagon train in 1872.

"They've made a hero out of that bird-brained phoney!" said Joe. "Why, he was too stupid to stay with the Army as an Indian scout. He led the Fourth Cavalry into so many ambushes the troopers figured he was half redskin and half blind."

Joe slapped twenty-five cents on the gasoline can.

"I want to hire you," he said. "My great-grandfather was wounded because of Buck Calhoun, and he had to retire from the Army. Prove Buck *wasn't* a hero! Then they'll have to tear down the statue of him."

"We can only do our best," said Encyclopedia carefully.

After the terrible-tempered Joe had left, Sally questioned Encyclopedia.

"Do you think we should have taken his money?" she asked. "This isn't an ordinary case.

Where do we begin?"

"At Fort Hope," said Encyclopedia. "Let's go."

Fort Hope stood eleven miles west of Idaville. The fort had been entirely rebuilt so that it looked exactly as it had looked in 1872.

As Encyclopedia and Sally got off the bus, they saw that the three o'clock tour of the fort was underway. A man in a black cap was guiding a small group of people to the many points of interest.

"Just in time!" said Encyclopedia.

The guide had stopped at the statue of Buck Calhoun. The detectives joined the group and listened to the tale of that desperate midnight in July, 1872.

"Buck Calhoun was a scout for the Fourth Cavalry before he became a famous wagon train master," began the guide. "Early in July, the Seminoles put on the war paint. Calhoun knew they were burning and scalping, and when he came through that mountain pass, he took a long, hard look at Fort Hope."

The guide turned and pointed to the mountain pass, which was now Emerson Avenue.

"Despite a light rain, Calhoun had a good view of the fort from up in the pass," went on the guide. "The American flag was flying proudly, and soldiers manned the walls. Everything looked all right."

The guide paused to allow the group to get the feeling of danger. Then he resumed.

"Calhoun was wagon-train master for five hundred settlers. Having studied the fort from the distance, he decided it was safe to move from the pass. So shortly after midnight he started down. Only he didn't know the truth. The redskins had slain everyone inside the fort. What Calhoun saw were Indians dressed up in the uniforms of the dead soldiers!"

A woman in the group let out a shriek of horror. The guide gave her a comforting look and went on.

"When the settlers got onto the open ground, the Indians poured out of the fort, hollering and whooping and shooting. Half the settlers were killed right off. The rest seemed doomed. But Calhoun stayed cool and did some fancy thinking. He closed up the big Conestoga wagons into columns of two's and raced for the fort's open gates."

A hush fell upon the group. No one moved. Everyone waited to hear the outcome of Buck Calhoun's heroic charge for the gates.

"Just as Calhoun figured," said the guide, "there wasn't enough room going through the gates for the skinniest Indian to sneak in alongside the big wagons. Suddenly all the settlers were inside the fort. And when Calhoun slammed the gates shut, all the Indians were outside. His courage, coolness, and quick thinking had saved half the settlers."

"You mean," spoke up Encyclopedia, "his stupidity *killed* half the settlers. He never should have led the wagon train down from the pass."

WHY NOT?

(*Turn to page 89 for the solution to the Case of the Wagon Master.*)

The Case of Sir Biscuit-Shooter

Lionel Fisk came into the Brown Detective Agency walking on his hands.

Encyclopedia knew what an upside-down Lionel meant. The circus was in town!

Lionel was the only boy in Idaville who wanted to be an acrobat. He could read an entire comic book while standing on his head.

"I brought you two tickets to the circus," he said, falling to his feet. "For you and Sally."

"Boy, thanks," said Encyclopedia. "They must have cost a lot."

Lionel shook his head. "My Uncle Barney sent them to me," he said proudly.

Encyclopedia knew about Lionel's Uncle

Barney. He had sold used cars, he had sold houses, and he had gone to prison for two years. Uncle Barney hadn't cheated people more than some men who sold used cars or houses. But he had been caught.

"Uncle Barney is working as a clown now," said Lionel. "After the show, I'll introduce you to him."

Lionel did five back flips and was out the door.

After lunch, Encyclopedia told Sally the good news. The partners caught the two o'clock bus to the circus grounds.

Lionel was there to greet them. He led them into the main tent and up the grandstand steps. The free seats were in the very last row. When the circus started, Encyclopedia scratched himself a few times. The center ring was so far away that even the elephants looked like trained fleas.

Lionel wriggled with delight when the clowns came on. His Uncle Barney first appeared as the rear end of a horse. Later, wearing pots and pans for armor, he clanked about as the fearless English knight, Sir Godfrey Biscuit-Shooter.

When the circus ended, Lionel took Encyclopedia and Sally behind the sideshow tents to meet Uncle Barney. Trailers, in which the performers lived and traveled, were parked in three rows.

"Hold it," said Encyclopedia suddenly. "There's some kind of trouble over there."

He pointed to a trailer with a lion's head painted on the side. A small group of circus people were gathered at the open door. Someone hollered, "Get the doctor!"

"And get that new clown Barney!" shouted Kitty, the bareback rider. She was dressed in a tight pink costume and soft slippers. "He's the one who did it!"

The three children moved toward the crowd. "Uncle Barney's in some kind of trouble," said Lionel in a worried tone.

As the doctor arrived, a woman in a housecoat stepped weakly from the trailer. She was holding her head.

"That's Princess Marta, the lion tamer," said Lionel. "She's the star of the show!"

The doctor helped Princess Marta into a folding chair. "What happened?" he asked.

"Somebody hit me on the head and stole my money," answered Princess Marta.

"Here's Barney," said the strongman, holding Uncle Barney by the neck.

The strongman shoved him, and Uncle Barney fell to the ground. His knight's costume of pots and pans banged loudly.

"He's the one who did it!" said Kitty. "I saw him slip out of the trailer a couple of minutes ago. How could I mistake him in that costume!"

"Come now, Kitty," said Princess Marta. "Everyone in the circus knows where I keep my money. The thief isn't one of us."

"Neither is Barney. He joined the show only last month," said the strongman.

"And he's been in prison, hasn't he?" said the sword swallower. "Look at him! He hasn't denied a word!"

Uncle Barney rose to his feet. Vainly he tried to quiet the pots and pans by pressing them against his body.

"I went by Princess Marta's trailer a few minutes ago," he said. "But I didn't go into it. I didn't steal her money."

"I believe him," said Princess Marta. She waved both arms for the crowd to go away.

"Hold still," said the doctor. "You've got a lump on your head bigger than a candy apple."

"What did the thief hit me with?" asked Princess Marta.

A midget held up a frying pan. "Probably with this," he said. "I found it just outside your trailer."

"Well, it isn't mine," said Princess Marta.

"It could be Barney's," said the midget. "He's got so many on him, you'd never know if one were missing."

"Barney's the thief, all right," said the strongman.

"Didn't you get a look at the thief?" asked the doctor.

"No," replied Princess Marta. "I never even heard him sneak in. I was sitting with my back to the door knitting. All of a sudden, *whomp!* The lights went out."

"Ah, what's the sense of talking," said the strongman. "Barney's the thief, all right." He seized Uncle Barney by the neck and shook him. "Where did you hide the money?"

"I didn't steal anything!" Uncle Barney protested. "You have to believe me!"

The crowd moved closer to him. There was a hum of ugly muttering.

"They're going to hurt him!" exclaimed Lionel.

"Encyclopedia," said Sally. "Can't you do something?"

"I can try," said Encyclopedia.

He stepped in front of Uncle Barney. "This man didn't steal your money," he said to Princess Marta.

Princess Marta regarded the boy detective with amused interest.

"If you're so sure he didn't rob me, tell me who did?" she said. "I expect you know that, too."

"Yes," answered Encyclopedia. "I do."

WHO WAS THE THIEF?

(*Turn to page 90 for the solution to the Case of Sir Biscuit-Shooter.*)

The Case of the Frightened Playboy

"That was Mr. Mackey," said Chief Brown as he hung up the telephone receiver.

"Goodness!" exclaimed Mrs. Brown. "Telephoning you at seven thirty in the morning! What is the matter with that man?"

"You know Mr. Mackey," said Chief Brown, seating himself at the breakfast table. "Every week he's afraid someone else is after his money."

"Two weeks ago he thought burglars were breaking into his house," said Mrs. Brown. "He called you at midnight!"

Encyclopedia had heard a lot about Mr. Mackey. Mr. Mackey's father owned five oil wells in Texas. So Mr. Mackey was very rich and did not have to work. He was Idaville's leading playboy.

"He ought to give all his money to the poor and get a job," said Mrs. Brown. "Then he wouldn't have to worry so much. What is he afraid of now? Kidnappers?"

"Last week he was afraid of kidnappers, remember?" Encyclopedia said.

"He thinks somebody is going to kill him," said Chief Brown. "He wouldn't tell me more over the telephone. So I said I'd stop by on my way to headquarters."

Encyclopedia immediately asked to go along. He had never met a millionaire.

"Is there any danger, dear?" Mrs. Brown asked anxiously.

"No, I'm sure Mr. Mackey is only crying wolf again," answered Chief Brown. "I think Leroy should go with me. He ought to see someone like Mr. Mackey—someone who let's his money run his life."

Mr. Mackey looked like he hadn't slept a wink in four years.

So Encyclopedia, after finishing breakfast, went with his father. It was eight o'clock when they got out of the patrol car at Mr. Mackey's house. A woman was standing by the front door.

"I've already rung the bell," she announced. She gave Chief Brown's police uniform a nervous look. "Is there trouble here? I came in answer to an ad for a maid. I won't work in a house where there is trouble!"

Before Chief Brown could reply, the door squeaked. It opened no more than a crack. Mr. Mackey peered out.

"Chief Brown!" he said. "Thank heaven you've come!"

He swung the door open. He was wearing slippers and pajamas, and he looked like he hadn't slept a wink in four years.

Chief Brown introduced Encyclopedia. Mr. Mackey smiled and shook hands. Then he noticed the woman.

"Who are you?" he demanded.

"I'm Molly Haggerty," she answered. "I've come about that job for a maid—"

"Oh, yes," said Mr. Mackey. "I forgot for the moment. Well, come in—come in."

Inside, Mr. Mackey said, "I'm sorry, Miss Haggerty, that I can't talk with you about the position now. I must speak with Chief Brown. But I'm hungry as a bear. Could I trouble you to fix something to eat? You'll find everything you need in the kitchen."

Molly Haggerty asked the way to the kitchen and strode off. Mr. Mackey led Chief Brown and Encyclopedia into the living room.

"Yesterday I put an ad in the newspaper for a maid," said Mr. Mackey. "I had to discharge my old one—caught her snooping! I can't trust anybody!"

"Do you live here alone?" asked Chief Brown.

"Yes, except for a maid—when I have one," said Mr. Mackey. "I hope this Molly Haggerty works out. She seems bright and eager to please."

Encyclopedia wondered about Mr. Mackey. Was he so all-fired scared simply because he had lost a maid?

"What is it you wanted to see me about?" inquired Chief Brown.

"Do you remember the gasoline station holdup last week in Allentown?" asked Mr. Mackey.

"Three gunmen held up the station and wounded the owner," recalled Chief Brown. "They go on trial tomorrow."

"And I'm going to appear in court against them," said Mr. Mackey.

"Why?"

"Because I saw what happened," replied Mr. Mackey. "I had stopped for gas, and I saw everything. I'm the only eyewitness."

Suddenly Chief Brown looked concerned. "You're afraid the gunmen's friends will try to keep you from appearing in court?"

"They'll kill me!" said Mr. Mackey fearfully. "I need a police guard day and night! Do you know how I've been living for the past week?"

Chief Brown shook his head. "How?"

"Like a mole—sneaking out at night!" said

Mr. Mackey. "During the day I live behind locked doors. I sleep during the morning and afternoon. I was out all last night walking—where's that maid? I'm starved. I want to eat and go to bed."

He had hardly spoken when Molly Haggerty entered the room. She was carrying a tray of food.

She set a bowl of soup, a sandwich, and a glass of ice tea on the end table by Mr. Mackey.

"Very nice, thank you," mumbled Mr. Mackey, picking up the sandwich hungrily.

Encyclopedia needed but a split second to see the clue.

"Don't eat!" he cried.

An instant later Chief Brown understood, too. He caught Molly Haggerty as she tried to escape by the back door. He put her under arrest.

"What's this all about?" cried Mr. Mackey.

"Miss Haggerty is a friend of the three gunmen who held up the gas station," answered Encyclopedia.

"H-how do you know?" gasped Mr. Mackey.

HOW DID ENCYCLOPEDIA KNOW?

(*Turn to page 91 for the solution to the Case of the Frightened Playboy.*)

The Case of the Hair Driers

Sally Kimball braked her bike to a skidding halt in front of the Brown Detective Agency.

"Fire!" she shouted excitedly. "The Glade Theater is on fire! Come on!"

Encyclopedia had never seen a theater burn. Since he was not working on a case, he closed the detective agency at once. He and Sally hopped on their bikes and rode quickly toward the center of town.

"Golly, I hope nobody is hurt," she said.

"It's only three o'clock," said Encyclopedia. "The first show doesn't start till five. The theater was probably empty when the fire started."

By the time they reached the theater, the fire had been put out. Most of the onlookers had moved away. The firemen were winding the hoses back on the fire engines.

The partners hung around watching the work. At last all the equipment was back in place. The fire engines drove off. Officer Wilson blew his whistle, waved, and traffic moved down the street again.

Encyclopedia and Sally walked their bikes on the sidewalk. In the middle of the block, Sally gave a gasp.

"Encyclopedia!"

A man had staggered from the alley between Mr. Albert's Shoe Store and the Sunset Five-and-Dime. He held his hands to his head.

It was Mr. Jorgens, who ran the beauty parlor on the corner, across the street from the theater.

At first Encyclopedia thought he had been hurt in the fire. But Mr. Jorgens moaned, "I've been robbed!" He slumped against a lamp post. "I've been robbed."

The two children guided Mr. Jorgens back to his beauty parlor. It was empty except for Mrs. Jorgens, who helped her husband run the business.

"I was slugged and robbed," said Mr. Jorgens to his wife.

Mrs. Jorgens gave a cry of fright. "Wh-who did it?"

"I don't know. That's the mystery," said Mr. Jorgens.

Mrs. Jorgens ran to get a doctor. Encyclopedia sent Sally to fetch Officer Wilson from the corner.

When Officer Wilson saw the lump on Mr. Jorgens's head, his first question was, "Are you able to tell me what happened?"

"I can talk," said Mr. Jorgens. "But I can't tell you very much. Somebody hit me from behind as I walked through the alley on the way to the bank. I never saw who it was."

"Do you usually go through the alley to get to the bank?" asked Officer Wilson.

"Yes, it's a shortcut," said Mr. Jorgens. "How-

The doctor examined Mr. Jorgens's head and frowned.

ever, I usually go on Fridays. I went today because I had more cash than I like to keep on hand."

"Whom did you tell that you were going to the bank today instead of Friday?" asked Officer Wilson.

"Only my wife," replied Mr. Jorgens.

At that moment Mrs. Jorgens returned with the doctor. He examined Mr. Jorgens's head and frowned. "You had better come to the hospital. I want to take X rays," he said.

"Can I have another minute to question him?" asked Officer Wilson.

"One minute," said the doctor. "No more."

"You said the only person who knew you were going to the bank today was your wife," said Officer Wilson. "Couldn't someone else have overheard you tell her?"

"They could have seen me, but they couldn't have overheard me." said Mr. Jorgens.

"What do you mean?"

"There were three customers here," said Mr. Jorgens. "They were sitting under those hair driers. The hair driers make so much noise that the three women couldn't have heard a word, even if I had shouted."

"Perhaps you were overheard by someone else—someone who works for you?" suggested Officer Wilson.

"I have only one assistant," said Mr. Jorgens. "Today is her day off."

"How long after you told Mrs. Jorgens that you were going to the bank today did you leave?"

"I told my wife about two o'clock," answered Mr. Jorgens. "It was shortly after the fire engines arrived at the theater. I left for the bank about two-thirty."

"And how much money was stolen?"

"Seven hundred and twenty dollars," said Mr. Jorgens.

Officer Wilson had carefully written everything down. He put his notebook away and thanked Mr. Jorgens. He went outside shaking his head, as though he believed the thief would never be caught.

Encyclopedia said nothing. He did not offer to solve the crime till the Browns sat down to dinner that evening.

Chief Brown brought up the case as he was finishing his mushroom soup.

"The only person who knew that Mr. Jorgens was going to the bank was his wife," he said. "She couldn't be guilty. The Jorgenses have been happily married for thirty years."

"It wasn't Mrs. Jorgens," said Encyclopedia.

"I know that," said Chief Brown. "But who was it?"

"It was one of the three women sitting under the hair driers," said Encyclopedia.

"Impossible!" objected Chief Brown. "The hair driers make too much noise. None of the women could have overheard Mr. Jorgens tell his wife about going to the bank."

"The guilty woman didn't overhear him, Dad," said Encyclopedia.

"Well, who did?" said Chief Brown.

"No one," said Encyclopedia. "That's what makes the case so simple."

"Leroy!" said his mother sharply. "Are you making a joke?"

"I'm not joking, Mom," said Encyclopedia. "All Dad has to do is find out which one of the three women is—"

IS WHAT?

(*Turn to page 92 for the solution to the Case of the Hair Driers.*)

The Case of Cupid's Arrow

Tyrone Taylor was the youngest ladies' man in Idaville. He was always holding some girl's hand.

But on the morning he entered the Brown Detective Agency, he was holding an arrow.

"Look what Cupid shot at me," he said. "Am I lucky he missed. Feel the point!"

Encyclopedia felt the point. It was sharp as a needle. "You could have been killed," he agreed.

"I want to hire you right away," said Tyrone, banging twenty-five cents on the gasoline can.

Encyclopedia did not touch the money. "You ought to write to Miss Lonely Hearts at the newspaper," he said. "She gives advice on love.

Cupid is out of my line."

"Maybe Cupid shot the arrow," said Tyrone, "or maybe a jealous rival is out to get me!"

"You stole someone's girl friend?" asked Encyclopedia.

"Certainly not," said Tyrone. "At the moment, I'm crazy over Ruth Goldstein. So is half the class. Some kid might be out to win her for himself by shooting all her other admirers. In a week, Idaville may look like the Indians raided it."

Encyclopedia pictured arrows flying and half the fifth grade wiped out. This was an emergency!

"I'll take the case," he said quickly. "Tell me what happened."

"Less than an hour ago I was sitting under a tree thinking about Ruth," said Tyrone. "I figured if I bought her a present, she'd think about me, too. But I'm broke. Then, all of a sudden—*pfff-lunk!* The arrow hit the tree right above my head."

Tyrone reached up. He pretended to pull the arrow from a tree.

"If I were three inches taller, I'd have been a goner," he said. "And if the arrow didn't get me, this diamond would have knocked me silly for a month."

From his pocket Tyrone pulled out a diamond. It was the biggest diamond Encyclopedia had ever seen.

"The diamond was tied to the arrow," said Tyrone. "The perfect gift for Ruth! See what I mean about Cupid?"

"You'd better show me where you were sitting," said Encyclopedia.

"I was sitting under one of Mr. Crane's trees," said Tyrone.

Mr. Crane was one of the richest men in Idaville. As the two boys came within sight of his big house, Tyrone stopped cold. "Police!" he yelped.

Three police cars were parked near the house.

Policemen were walking about, searching the grounds.

"I don't want to get mixed up with the police," Tyrone said. "I'm really not a lover at heart— I'm a coward." He shoved the arrow and the diamond into Encyclopedia's hands and fled.

The next instant Encyclopedia heard his father calling.

"I'm glad to see you, Leroy," Chief Brown said quietly. "We've got a bit of a mystery here."

Then he told Encyclopedia about the events of the morning at Mr. Crane's house.

Mr. Crane owned the Greenwood Diamond, one of the largest and most valuable diamonds in the world. About an hour ago he had been alone in the house. He heard someone force open a window.

Fearing a thief, Mr. Crane raced to his study. He removed the diamond from its glass showcase. Then he took down a bow and arrow which hung on the wall. He tied the diamond to the arrow and ran to the back staircase.

Halfway up the narrow flight of stairs was a landing with a window. Mr. Crane opened the window, fitted the arrow to the bow, and waited.

Soon a masked man appeared at the bottom of the staircase. He realized how Mr. Crane intended to keep the diamond from him. He ran up the stairs, but he was too late. Mr. Crane had already fired the arrow with the diamond out the window.

Enraged, the masked man beat Mr. Crane with his fists before escaping.

"Mr. Crane is in the hospital. Luckily, he's not seriously hurt," said Chief Brown. "He thinks the thief may have been Mr. Holt. For two years, Mr. Holt has tried to buy the diamond, and recently he has become ugly and threatening."

"Have you questioned Mr. Holt?" asked Encyclopedia.

"Not yet—I'm having him picked up and brought here," replied Chief Brown. "The trou-

*Encyclopedia brought the arrow and the diamond
from behind his back.*

ble is that the thief—Mr. Holt or whoever he was—found the diamond."

"No he didn't," said Encyclopedia. "Tyrone Taylor found it." He brought the arrow and the diamond from behind his back and explained about Tyrone.

Then he said, "If Mr. Holt was the masked man, I think I have a plan to trap him."

Encyclopedia unfolded his plan as Chief Brown put the arrow and diamond in his patrol car. Father and son were standing at the bottom of the narrow back staircase when Mr. Holt was brought in by Officer Parks.

"What's the meaning of this?" demanded Mr. Holt.

Chief Brown said, "Mr. Crane was beaten up this morning by a masked man. His Greenwood Diamond is missing. Were you in this house this morning?"

"No!" retorted Mr. Holt. "And I have no idea what this is all about. But if the diamond is missing, find it. I want to buy it!"

Chief Brown stared at the narrow staircase. "The diamond won't be hard to find," he said. "It's only an arrow flight away."

"Then what are you standing there for?" shouted Mr. Holt. "Go outside and hunt for it!"

"Put him under arrest," Chief Brown snapped to Officer Parks.

After Mr. Holt was dragged away, Chief Brown said, "Your plan worked fine, Leroy."

HOW HAD ENCYCLOPEDIA TRAPPED MR. HOLT?

(*Turn to page 93 for the solution to the Case of Cupid's Arrow.*)

The Case of the Wounded Dog

When Encyclopedia solved a case at the dinner table, his father usually gave him the evening off.

Encyclopedia had just solved the holdup of the Denton Supermarket over roast beef and fried mashed potato balls. As he dug into a slice of upside-down cake, he felt free to relax.

But Chief Brown had a second case.

"There's been trouble again with Pinky Plummer's dog Rex," he said.

Pinky Plummer was one of Encyclopedia's closest pals, and Rex was a neighborhood favorite. Nobody had ever complained about the little dog. Nobody, that is, except Mr. Harwood, who had moved next door to the Plummers last month.

"Rex has been digging up Mr. Harwood's rose beds again," said Chief Brown. "Mr. Harwood called headquarters this afternoon. He demanded that Rex be locked up."

"Gosh, Dad, is that a case for the *police?*"

"I don't want it to become one," said his father. "I thought I'd pay both the Plummers and the Harwoods a visit tonight. Perhaps I can head off serious trouble between them."

Chief Brown leaned back in his chair.

"I'd like you to come along, Leroy," he said thoughtfully. "You're a good friend of Pinky's."

Of course, Encyclopedia said he would go. Getting mixed up in the problems of grown-ups, however, wasn't something he especially liked.

After helping his mother clear the table and wash the dishes, he got ready. He put on a clean shirt and flicked a wet comb through his hair.

Then he got into the patrol car with his father.

It was eight o'clock when they drew near Pinky's house. Night was down. The lights from the houses threw shadows across the street and lawns.

Suddenly four reports sounded near Mr. Harwood's house.

"Those were gunshots!" said Chief Brown.

"Look!" exclaimed Encyclopedia.

Mr. Harwood was standing on the sidewalk in front of his house. He held a gun in his right hand.

Seconds later the street came alive. Families ran out of their houses to see what was going on.

Chief Brown jumped from the patrol car. He had his pistol drawn.

"There was a robber in my house!" said Mr. Harwood. "Right in my study! I fired at him, but he got away!"

As Chief Brown began questioning Mr. Harwood, the Plummer family walked over from

Pinky gave a cry and dropped to his knees.

next door. Pinky gave a cry and dropped to his knees. Rex was lying in the shadows, whimpering softly.

The little dog was wounded in the leg.

"You shot my dog!" cried Pinky.

His eyes filled with tears. He leaped up and ran at Mr. Harwood. His father caught him and held him back.

Several neighbors moved nearer Mr. Harwood. They were in an angry mood.

"I shot at a robber," Mr. Harwood insisted. "I didn't mean to hurt the dog. I didn't even see him."

Mr. Plummer picked Rex up carefully. "He'll be all right," he said, trying to comfort Pinky.

"You people go back to your homes," Chief Brown told the onlookers. "Go on, now."

When the street was cleared, Chief Brown introduced Encyclopedia to Mr. Harwood.

"So this is the boy who runs a detective agency," said Mr. Harwood. He chuckled and patted Encyclopedia on the head. "Come inside. I'll show you where I saw the robber."

He led the way into his house and stopped in a room walled with bookcases. In the center of the room was a desk and chair, and behind these stood a large easy chair and a reading lamp. A newspaper lay on the carpet by the lamp.

"I live with my sister," said Mr. Harwood. "It's a small house, and I spend most evenings here in the study."

Encyclopedia walked to the open window. The ground was only three feet below.

"My sister is visiting friends tonight," said Mr. Harwood. "I was alone in the house. I was reading the newspaper in the easy chair, and I expect I dozed off. Suddenly a noise awoke me. A masked man was going through my desk."

Mr. Harwood sat down in the easy chair. He reached back to his right and noiselessly opened a cabinet built below a bookcase. He took out a box and opened it. He put the gun he had been carrying into the box and replaced the box in the cabinet. Finally, he closed the cabinet door. He did all this without making a sound.

"The gun belonged to my grandfather, and I treasure it," he said.

"You were seated like this when you awoke and saw the robber?" said Chief Brown. "Then what did you do?"

"Luckily, the robber had his back to me," said Mr. Harwood. "I was able to open the cabinet and take out the gun without his hearing me. I told him to put up his hands. Instead, he hit me and fled through the window."

"Did you chase him?" asked Chief Brown.

"Yes, out to the front lawn," answered Mr. Harwood. "I fired four shots at him. I was a bit dazed from his blow, and I'm afraid I probably missed all four. An instant later you drove up. That's all there is to tell."

"I'd like to look around outside," said Chief Brown.

When he was alone outside with Encyclopedia, Chief Brown said, "Well, what do you think, Leroy?"

"Mr. Harwood tried to kill Rex," said Encyclopedia. "When we drove up unexpectedly and saw him holding the gun, he had to make up the story about a robber!"

HOW DID ENCYCLOPEDIA KNOW?

(Turn to page 94 for the solution to the Case of the Wounded Dog.)

The Case of the Earthenware Pig

"The cops are after me!"

The words came out of a blur. Something that looked like Charlie Stewart in fast motion sped through the Brown Detective Agency and disappeared into the tool closet.

Encyclopedia glanced up and down the street.

"There isn't a policeman in sight," he announced. "You gave them the slip."

The news failed to cheer Charlie. Opening the closet door a crack," he moaned, "I'm a wanted man!"

"Wanted for what?" asked Encyclopedia.

"How should I know?" said Charlie. "Five minutes ago I was walking down Locust Street.

I came to the outdoor telephone booth at the corner of Locust and Beech, and there stood Bugs Meany and Officer Carlson. Bugs pointed at me and hollered, 'Arrest that kid!' I got scared and ran."

Charlie tiptoed out of the tool closet.

"I think this has something to do with my tooth collection," he said.

Charlie's tooth collection was the pride of Idaville. No boy anywhere in the state had collected more interesting uppers and lowers than Charlie. He kept them in a flowered cookie jar.

"Bugs owns an earthenware teapot shaped like a pig," Charlie continued thoughtfully. "He wanted to trade it for my tooth collection. I don't drink tea. So I told him no soap."

"What could Bugs want with your tooth collection?" asked Encyclopedia.

"Bugs was going to string the teeth behind the Tiger clubhouse," answered Charlie. "If anybody tried to sneak upon the clubhouse from the rear, he'd trip over the string. The string would

"I told you we'd find the little thief here!" sang Bugs.

shake, and the teeth would start chattering and warn the Tigers."

"Wow, dental detectors!" exclaimed Encyclopedia. "Pretty neat. I have to hand it to Bugs—"

Encyclopedia's voice trailed off. A police car had pulled into the Brown driveway. Bugs Meany hopped out, followed by Officer Carlson.

"I told you we'd find the little thief here!" sang Bugs. "I always knew this detective business was just a cover for a den of crooks!"

Officer Carlson motioned Bugs to be quiet. Then he said to Charlie, "Why were you walking on Locust Street about five minutes ago?"

"I got a telephone call to come there," replied Charlie. "A boy's voice asked me to meet him at the telephone booth right away. He said he had two grizzly bear teeth to sell. He wouldn't give his name."

"Yah, yah, yah!" jeered Bugs. "You were on your way to buy grizzly bear teeth! So how come the second you saw Officer Carlson you made like a drum and beat it?"

"B-because y-you hollered for him to arrest me," Charlie said. "I got plain scared."

"Stop it, you two," said Officer Carlson. "Bugs says you stole an earthenware teapot shaped like a pig, Charlie. Did you?"

"I did not!" said Charlie. And looking hard at Bugs he added, "I don't like pigs!"

As Bugs turned a lovely shade of purple, Officer Carlson held up his hand. "Let's all go to Bugs's house and try to find out what really happened."

Walking toward the police car, Charlie slipped Encyclopedia twenty-five cents. "I'll need you," he whispered. "I've never been in trouble with the police before."

At his house, Bugs stopped in the entrance hall.

"My folks have gone for the day," he said. He pointed to the staircase on his left. "I'd just come home when Charlie raced down the stairs. He had my teapot pig under his arm. I chased him out the front door, but he got away."

"Why couldn't you catch him?" inquired

Encyclopedia. "You're bigger, older, and faster."

"Why?" said Bugs. "I'll tell you why, Mr. Brains. I obey the law. There was a green light over at Locust Street, and I don't cross against the green. "I'm no jaywalker!"

"He's lying like a tiger skin," muttered Charlie.

Officer Carlson said, "Let's say Charlie did cross against the light and got away. What did you do next, Bugs?"

"I went straight to the telephone booth on the corner and called the police station," said Bugs. "I waited there till you arrived."

"You told me," said Officer Carlson, "that the cabinet in which you keep the teapot pig is always locked. You said the thief removed the hinges of the cabinet door to get inside it."

"Yeah," said Bugs. "It was a slick job. Charlie sure knew what he was doing." He led the way upstairs to his room.

The cabinet stood in a corner. The glass door, lifted off its hinges, was leaning against the wall.

"There," said Bugs. "Just like I said."

"But Charlie wasn't carrying the teapot pig when we saw him coming toward the telephone booth," pointed out Officer Carlson.

"He had plenty of time to hide it," said Bugs. "Then he tried to bluff you with that nutty story about buying grizzly bear teeth at the telephone booth. He had his alibi all ready!"

Officer Carlson regarded Charlie sternly. "I better call your parents," he said.

"Aw, I don't want him sent to prison or nothing," said Bugs. "I'm the kind that's always ready to forgive and forget. Charlie's been after me for weeks to swap my teapot pig for his tooth collection. I'll tell you what. If he's so crazy for my teapot, he can keep it. I'll take his crumby old tooth collection in trade."

"You won't take anything of Charlie's," said Encyclopedia. "He never stole your teapot pig!"

WHAT MADE ENCYCLOPEDIA SO SURE?

(*Turn to page 95 for the solution to the Case of the Earthenware Pig.*)

The Case of the Muscle Maker

Cadmus Turner stopped and glared at the large tree outside the Brown Detective Agency. His lips curled.

"Arrahhrrr!" he snarled.

He crouched, circled to his left, and attacked without warning. He threw both arms about the tree and began wrestling it.

Encyclopedia had never seen Cadmus so full of fight. He hurried out to the sidewalk for a ringside view.

The bout lasted a minute—till Cadmus's pants fell down. He let go of the tree at once.

"It's a gyp!" he hollered. "I've been robbed."

"It looked like a fair fight till your pants

quit," said Encyclopedia. "Next time you tussle the timber, tighten your belt first. You'll win for sure."

"I can't tighten my belt," replied Cadmus. "The ends don't meet any more. I drank four bottles of Hercules's Strength Tonic. I'm ready to bust."

Encyclopedia eyed Cadmus's stomach. It was swollen out like the start of a new continent.

"I should have been able to tear that tree off its roots," said Cadmus.

"Because you drank four bottles of Hercules's Strength Tonic?" asked Encyclopedia.

"Yep," said Cadmus. "Only the stuff doesn't work. I was supposed to feel like Hercules. Instead I feel like a fat slob. And I'm out two dollars!"

"I might get your money back," said Encyclopedia, "if I can prove the tonic is a fake."

"You're hired," said Cadmus. "But I spent all my cash on those four bottles of wish-water. I'll have to pay you later."

Encyclopedia agreed to take the case on faith. Considering the blown-up condition of Cadmus's stomach, it was more an act of mercy than a business deal.

The boys biked to an unused fruit stand on Pine Drive. Cadmus had bought the bottles there earlier that morning.

"Two big kids were setting out boxes of the tonic," said Cadmus. "They told me if I became their first customer, I could have four bottles for the price of two."

"You couldn't say no to a bargain like that," commented Encyclopedia with understanding.

At the fruit stand, a large crowd of children was assembled. Bugs Meany and his Tigers had pushed their way to the front.

The two big boys were about to start the sale. Encyclopedia recognized one of them. He was Wilford Wiggins, a high school dropout. Wilford had more get-rich-quick ideas than tail feathers on a turkey farm. The other boy, a husky youth, was a stranger.

"He's Mike O'Malley," said Cadmus, "from Homestead."

"He looks like he's from Fort Apache," said Encyclopedia. Mike's suit, though it fit perfectly, was wrinkled enough to have gone through an Indian war.

"Gather 'round," shouted Wilford Wiggins. He waved a bottle of Hercules's Strength Tonic. "Gather 'round."

His partner, Mike O'Malley, dropped to the ground and began doing push-ups like a trip-hammer.

"Would you believe Mike weighed only one hundred pounds a year ago?" asked Wilford. "They called him Ribs."

Mike jumped up and removed his suitcoat and shirt. Bare chested, he made muscles in all directions.

"In one short year," bellowed Wilford, "Mike gained a hundred pounds of solid muscle! A miracle, you say? Yes, that's what Hercules's

Bare chested, Mike made muscles in all directions.

Strength Tonic is—a miracle. The same secret miracle tonic can build a mighty body for each and every boy here today—if," he added hastily, noticing Cadmus and his stomach—"if taken as directed."

Mike was wriggling his huge chest muscles. The battleship tattooed over his heart rolled and pitched.

"See that battleship?" asked Wilford. "Why, a year ago it was nothing but a rowboat! Ahah, hah, hah!"

Bugs Meany held his nose at the joke. "How come you have to sell this wash on the street?" he demanded. "If it's so good, you could sell it in stores."

"A fair question, friend," said Wilford. "I'll give you an honest answer. We need money. We're broke."

Wilford held up Mike's wrinkled suit coat.

"Take a look at this suit coat," Wilford said. "Old and shabby, isn't it? Mike's worn it for two years. Why? Because he didn't think about spending money on himself. He thought only of the powerful body he was going to give every skinny, weak-kneed little shrimp in America!"

Wilford put down the suit coat. He picked up a bottle of Hercules's Strength Tonic again.

"Every cent we had went into developing Mike's wonderful tonic," Wilford continued. "We need money to get the tonic into every store in America! It's a crusade! So I'm cutting the price. You can have four bottles—that's all you need—for half the regular price. Four bottles for a measly two dollars!"

"And I thought he was giving *me* a special price," Cadmus said angrily.

"Forget it," said Encyclopedia. "Look at Bugs."

The Tigers' leader was pop-eyed watching Mike's arm muscles lump, jump, and bump.

"How do you take this tonic," Bugs asked eagerly.

"One teaspoonful a day," replied Wilford. "Four big bottles like this one will last twelve months. Then you'll have a build like Mike's!"

"I couldn't wait a year," Cadmus muttered. "So I drank the four bottles one after the other. Maybe the stuff works if you follow the directions."

"It doesn't work," said Encyclopedia. "Mike's muscles and Wilford's big sales talk prove it's a fake!"

HOW DID ENCYCLOPEDIA KNOW?

(*Turn to page 96 for the solution to the Case of the Muscle Maker.*)

Solution to *the Case of the Missing Clues*

Encyclopedia did not find the clues he was looking for—cherry stems and cherry pits!

Had Bugs been "in the clubhouse all afternoon, eating cherries" which he had bought at the supermarket, as he claimed, the pits and stems would have been there, too!

Beaten once again by Encyclopedia, Bugs admitted he had taken the cherries from Abner's fresh-fruit stand. He had eaten most of them on the way to the clubhouse.

Bugs also admitted that Abner's fruit stand had never been in danger. His protection service was just an excuse to get fruit without paying for it.

Bugs paid Abner for all the fruit he had eaten during the past two weeks.

Then he retired from the protection business.

Solution to *the Case of the Super-Secret Hold*

Bugs tried to scare Sally with his super-secret hold.

All the children but Encyclopedia believed that Spike and Rocky were really put to sleep, and that they could have been seriously hurt if Bugs had wanted to hurt them.

Encyclopedia alone saw that Spike and Rocky weren't really knocked out.

He whispered to Sally the reason he knew they were only faking.

Spike and Rocky had fallen over on their backs.

A person who is knocked senseless, or who loses consciousness while standing up, does not fall backward.

He falls forward.

Solution to *the Case of the Wagon Master*

After capturing Fort Hope, the Indians left the American flag flying. They did not know there were rules for displaying it.

But Buck Calhoun had been a scout for the Fourth Cavalry. He should have known how to honor the flag.

Before coming down from the pass, he saw the flag flying. He thought this meant that everything was all right at the fort.

He had never learned that the flag is not flown after sunset under normal conditions, or in the rain.

That it was flying in the rain at midnight should have instantly warned him that something was wrong at the fort!

P.S. The statue of Buck Calhoun was taken away.

Solution to *the* Case of *Sir Biscuit-Shooter*

Princess Marta said she hadn't heard the thief enter her trailer.

That proved Uncle Barney was innocent, since he could not have entered her trailer without being heard. He wore his knight's costume of pots and pans. The rattling and clanking would have given him away!

Yet the bareback rider, Kitty, claimed she saw him come out of the trailer.

So Kitty had lied. And Encyclopedia saw that her "soft slippers" made it possible for *her* to enter the trailer silently.

Outwitted by the boy detective, Kitty confessed. She had stolen the money. She had blamed the crime on Uncle Barney because he had been in prison, and so people would be ready to believe him guilty.

Solution to *the Case of the Frightened Playboy*

Encyclopedia realized that Molly Haggerty knew too much about Mr. Mackey to be just a maid.

She knew he went out at night and slept during the day!

Seeing Mr. Mackey in his pajamas and slippers at eight o'clock in the morning, a maid would have brought him cereal, fruit and toast—that is, *breakfast*.

But Molly Haggerty had brought a light *supper!*

Having trapped herself, she confessed. With other friends of the three gunmen who held up the gasoline station, she had been watching Mr. Mackey for days. She had answered his ad for a maid in order to slip sleeping powder into his food. Mr. Mackey was to be kept hidden till after the trial of the three gunmen.

Solution to *the Case of the Hair Driers*

"—deaf!"

Since the hair driers drowned out every other noise, the guilty woman couldn't have overheard what was said.

But like most deaf persons, she could read lips!

She read Mr. Jorgens's lips when he told his wife about taking the money to the bank.

The next day Chief Brown found out that one of the three women, Mrs. O'Brien, was deaf. She confessed.

She had read Mr. Jorgens's lips. With everyone watching the fire, she knew the alley would be empty. She had hidden behind some boxes till Mr. Jorgens walked past. Then she had hit him on the head with a piece of wood and stolen his money.

Solution to *the Case of Cupid's Arrow*

Chief Brown said what Encyclopedia had asked him to say about where the diamond was. That is, "It's only an arrow flight away."

Mr. Holt answered, "Go outside and hunt for it!"

Had Mr. Holt been innocent, he would have answered, "Go *upstairs* and hunt for it!"

An innocent man would not have known about the bow and arrow. So he would have heard Chief Brown say, "It's only *a narrow* flight away," and not, "It's only *an arrow* flight away."

Just before he spoke, Chief Brown had stared at the narrow flight of stairs, remember? An innocent man would have thought Chief Brown meant the flight of stairs when he said "flight," not the flight of an arrow!

Solution to the Case of the Wounded Dog

Once Mr. Harwood had taken out the gun, he would not have:

1. Put the empty gun box back in the cabinet.
2. Closed the cabinet door.
3. *Then* told the robber to raise his hands.

He would have dropped the box and left the cabinet door open in his eagerness to capture the robber.

Yet the box was in the cabinet and the cabinet door was closed when he told his story to Chief Brown and Encyclopedia.

Faced with this weakness in his story, Mr. Harwood told the truth. There had been no robber. He had really tried to kill Rex.

Rex recovered. By then, Mr. Harwood had moved from Idaville.

Solution to *the Case of the Earthenware Pig*

According to his own story, Bugs chased Charlie out of the house. Furthermore, he did not go upstairs to his room where the cabinet was until he brought back Officer Carlson, Charlie, and Encyclopedia.

Yet he knew how the cabinet had been opened!

He could not have known whether the lock had been forced, or the glass door broken, or the hinges removed—unless he had been the "thief" himself!

When Encyclopedia pointed out his mistake, Bugs confessed. He had tried to make it look as if Charlie were the thief in order to get Charlie's tooth collection.

The Tiger leader admitted he had been the boy who had lured Charlie to the telephone booth with the offer of selling him grizzly bear teeth. He had wanted Charlie to tell a story so unbelievable that Officer Carlson would think Charlie was guilty.

Solution to *the Case of the Muscle Maker*

Wilford Wiggins tried to make the children believe Mike had gained a hundred pounds in one year by drinking Hercules's Strength Tonic.

He also tried to make them believe Mike had been unable to buy a suit because all his money went into developing the tonic.

But the old suit coat still "fit perfectly" on Mike.

If Mike had really gained a hundred pounds in one year, he would have outgrown the suit coat!

When Encyclopedia pointed out this fact to the crowd of children, Wilford had to stop the sale.

And he returned Cadmus's two dollars.